VOLUME TWO

All stories PLOTTED by Ryan Brown and Dean Clarrain
and WRITTEN by Dean Clarrain

PENCILS by Ken Mitchroney and Jim Lawson

INKS by Dan Berger and Gary Fields

COLORS by Steve Lavigne with Michael Gaydos
and assisted by Denise St.Laurent-Lavigne

LETTERING by Gary Fields

COVER by Ken Mitchroney, Ryan Brown and Steve Lavigne

The Collected Teenage Mutant Ninja Turtles Adventures, Volume Two, is published by Tundra Publishing Ltd., 320 Riverside Drive, Northampton, MA 01060 and is Copyright © 1990, 1991 by Mirage Studios, P.O. Box 417, Haydenville, MA 01039, unless otherwise noted. This volume primarily reprints stories that originally appeared in Teenage Mutant Ninja Turtles Adventures published by Archie Comic Publications, Inc. Any similarity to any person living or dead or any institution, published in this volume, is, except for satirical purposes, entirely coincidental.

ISBN: 1-879450-04-6

1

3

4

5

...AND THEN TAKE A STORM DRAIN...

..DOWN TO THE SEWERS.

KLANK!

THE FORCE OF THIS CURRENT IS AMAZING!

THINK OF IT AS A JACUZZI.

NOT ME! I'M TOO BUSY THINKING ABOUT THOSE MILKWEED AND APPLE-CORE MICROWAVE PIZZAS WAITING FOR US BACK HOME!

WHAT A CHEESE-HEAD!

WE'RE HOME.

6

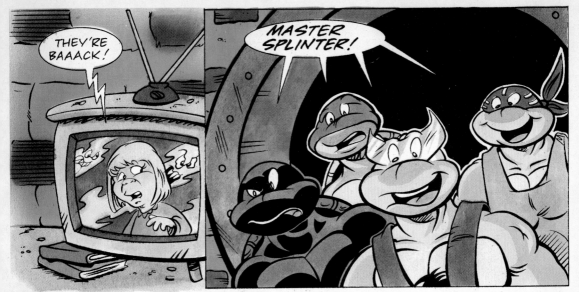

THEY'RE BAAACK!

MASTER SPLINTER!

BRUCE LEE

WELCOME...

...MY SONS.

CLICK

ZIK!

I WAS JUST WATCHING... ≥AHEM≤ THE NEWS.

...ARE CALLING IT THE WORST *TROPICAL STORM* TO STRIKE THE NEW YORK METROPOLITAN AREA IN FIVE YEARS.

HAPPY HOUR NEWS

HEY! APRIL'S AN ANCHOR!

YOU'VE BEEN FAR.

WHY, *YES*, MASTER, WE WERE *ABDUCTED* INTO SPACE BY INTERGALACTIC WRESTLING PROMOTERS AND *FORCED* TO WRESTLE!

ALIENS.

I SEE.

SO HOW DID YOU FARE?

WE WON.

AND THE LESSON LEARNED?

HEY, CHECK THIS OUT.

HOUR NEWS

...OVER A *THOUSAND SKYLIGHTS* ACROSS THE CITY HAVE BEEN *BROKEN* TONIGHT...

BROKEN... BY STONES THROWN BY AN *UNKNOWN HAND.*

ALTHOUGH UNABLE TO DETERMINE THE *CAUSE* OF THIS VANDALISM, AUTHORITIES SAY A FULL-SCALE INVESTIGATION IS "UNDER WAY." WE'LL BE RIGHT BACK AFTER THIS *MESSAGE* FROM ONE OF OUR *SPONSORS.*

8

HEE! HEE-HEE! HEEHEEHEEHEE...

A CRAZED BAT-LIKE CREATURE WHO...

WAY TO GO, BOSS! HAVE A ROCK!

HEH!

WHO...

HA HA HA HA HA HA

SWOOSH

ZING!

UH-OH.

FZZT!

GEE, DO YOU THINK THE AUTHORITIES HAVE FIGURED OUT WHO BROKE THE SKYLIGHTS YET?

WE'VE GOT TO STOP THEM!

THE BLIMP! LET'S USE OUR BLIMP!

SOUNDS LIKE A PLAN. LET'S GO!

YEAH!

WE'RE OUTTA HERE!

YOUTH.

SLAM!

11

14

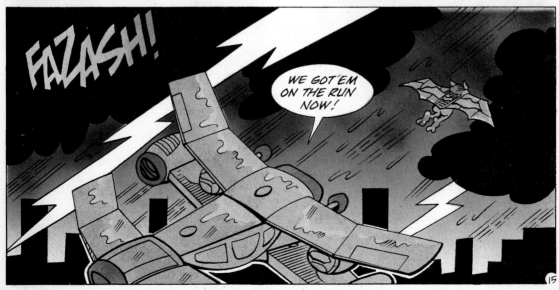

15

16

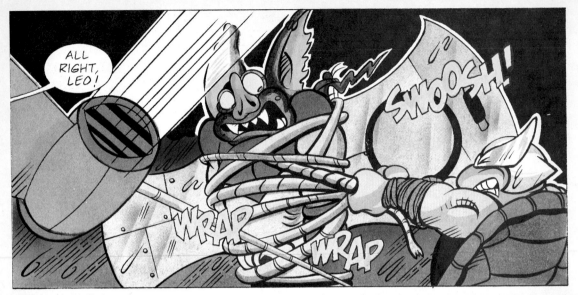

WINGNUT IS FROM *HUANU*, A PLANET WITH A PERPETUAL RED NIGHT...

WINGNUT LIVED HAPPILY WITH HIS PARENTS. HE WAS THEIR ONLY CHILD.

NOT LONG AGO, ALIEN INVADERS CAME TO CONQUER HUANU...

ZABAF!

ZOOM!

WINGNUT'S PARENTS WERE KILLED AT THE BEGINNING OF THE INVASION, AS WERE MOST OF HIS PEOPLE.

ZAP!

ZORCH!!

MOM! POP!

WITH ALL OF ITS FEMALES DEAD, HIS RACE IS DOOMED TO CERTAIN *EXTINCTION*.

MAYBE NOW YOU CAN UNDERSTAND THE *SOURCE* OF THE BOSS' INSANITY...

HE PROBABLY WOULDN'T HAVE MADE IT THIS FAR..., IF IT WASN'T FOR *ME*.

24

PATOOIE!

HERE ARE YOUR UNIFORMS. YOU LEFT THEM RINGSIDE AT STUMP ARENA.

THANKS. ARE YOU TAKING WINGNUT AND SCREWLOOSE *HOME*?

NOT HOME, MICHAEL. THEY NO LONGER HAVE A HOME.

MISTER STUMP HAS SHOWN AN *INTEREST* IN THESE TWO... SO WE'RE OFF TO *STUMP ASTEROID.*

AGAINST THEIR *WILL*?

MISTER STUMP HAS HIS *PLANS...*

ELSETIME, TURTLES.

YOU'D THINK THERE'D BE *LAWS* AGAINST INTER-DIMENSIONAL *KIDNAPPING.*

27

SATURDAY MORNING, TURTLE HEADQUARTERS,. SOMEWHERE DEEP WITHIN MANHATTAN'S SEWERS.

MY SONS, HOW LONG HAS IT BEEN SINCE YOU'VE PATROLLED THE SEWERS?

DID YOU *HEAR* SOMETHING, MICHAELANGELO?

NOPE, NOT A THING.

MASTER SPLINTER IS RIGHT...

AND BESIDES, MAYBE WE CAN PICK UP SOME *GROCERIES* WHILE WE'RE OUT.

OBOY!

WONDERFUL.

LET'S *MOTIVATE*, BROTHERS.

EVERYONE GET THEIR WEAPONS...

SWORDS, SAIS, NUNCHUKUS, STAFF, SHURIKEN...

DON'T FORGET TO PICK UP PLENTY OF CHEESE.

... AND WE'RE *OUTTA HERE!*

2

SLAM!

HEADLONG INTO THE FUTURE, HEEDLESS OF *TODAY*.

YOUTH.

AND *WHAT* IS HAPPENING IN *THIS* WORLD TODAY?

KLIK!

VEGAVIEW TECHNICOLOR

--OFFICERS HAVE *YET* TO ARRIVE AT AN EXPLANATION FOR THE VANDALISM LEADING TO THE DESTRUCTION OF OVER *ONE THOUSAND SKYLIGHTS* LAST EVENING.

ELSEWHERE IN THE CITY TODAY A *POLICE MANHUNT* IS UNDERWAY FOR A *DOUBLE AGENT* BELIEVED TO HAVE STOLEN *CLASSIFIED WEAPONS PLANS* FROM THE *TOP SECRET* FILES OF THE *UNITED NATIONS*.

Top Secret

THE DOUBLE AGENT, KNOWN ONLY BY THE CODENAME OF *CHAMELEON*, IS BELIEVED TO HAVE GAINED ACCESS TO THE U.N. FILES BY POSING AS A UNITED STATES *DIPLOMAT*.

CHAMELEON WAS LAST SEEN ESCAPING ON-FOOT IN THE VICINITY OF *TIMES SQUARE*. IT IS NOT KNOWN IF HE IS *ARMED*.

THE *WEAPONS PLANS* ARE SAID TO BE--

3

--OF VITAL IMPORTANCE TO THE MAINTENANCE OF *WORLD PEACE.*

..BUT IT IS SAID TO BE MORE *"PROFOUND"* THAN THE MOST POWERFUL INTER-CONTINENTAL BALLISTIC MISSILES CURRENTLY EMPLOYED BY EITHER THE SOVIET UNION OR THE UNITED STATES.

THE EXACT *WEAPON TYPE* IS NOT KNOWN..

AUTHORITIES HAVE LENT PARTICULAR *URGENCY* TO THIS MAN-HUNT--

--LEST THE PLANS FALL INTO THE *WRONG HANDS.*

"WRONG HANDSZ"

HA HA HA HA HA

I WANT THOSE WEAPONS PLANS AND I WANT THEM *NOW!*

BEBOP-- ROCKSTEADY--

DUH-YEAH, MISTA SHREDDAZ

4

7

OUCH.

HOW STRANGE...

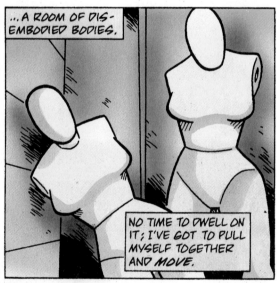

...A ROOM OF DIS-EMBODIED BODIES.

NO TIME TO DWELL ON IT; I'VE GOT TO PULL MYSELF TOGETHER AND *MOVE*.

NEED TO FIND A PLACE TO HOLE-UP, A PLACE WHERE IT'LL BE SAFE TO GATHER MY THOUGHTS... TO *PLAN*.

BASEMENT →

AND I KNOW JUST *WHERE* TO GO...

...DOWN UNDER.

WISH I HADN'T WORN MY BEST TUX.

SEWERS... YUCK.

8

WOW--LOOK AT ALL THE *NEAT STUFF* FLOATING IN THE SEWER!

THERE'S A DEFLATED *BALLOON*... SOMETHING *PLASTIC*...

A *HAMBURGER WRAPPER*...

AN *APPLE CORE*...WHAT MIGHT BE A *CHOCOLATE BAR*...

LAY OFF IT, DONATELLO. YOU'RE MAKING ME HUNGRY.

YOU GUYS ARE SUCH *STOMACH-HEADS!*

9

10

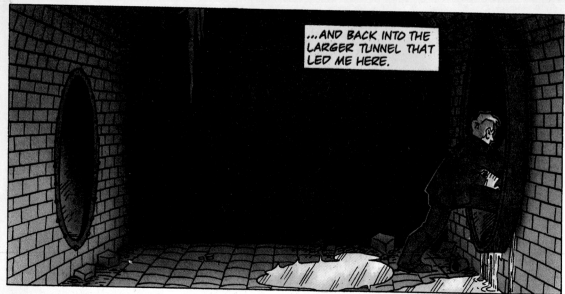

...AND BACK INTO THE LARGER TUNNEL THAT LED ME HERE.

WHAT?

DUH, WHAT'S DIS GUY LOOK LIKE ANYWAY?

WASN'T YOU PAYING ATTENTION TO DA TV WHEN IT SHOWED HIS PITCHER?

DUH, NO. I WUZ HELPING YOU SCREW IN DAT DERE LIGHTBULB.

VOICES APPROACHING FROM *THIS* DIRECTION, TOO?

CAN'T GO *BACK*.

CAN'T GO *FORWARD*.

GEEZ, WELL, HE KINDA LOOKS LIKE...

I'D BETTER *STASH* THE STOLEN PLANS...

...SINCE IT LOOKS LIKE I'M *STUCK* RIGHT HERE IN THE *MIDDLE*...

13

14

WHACK!

OOF!

WAM!

OW!

HEE-YAH!

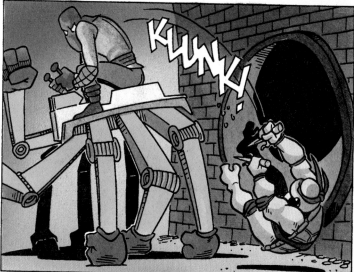

KLUNK!

LEO-- IT'S A ROBOT!

A ROBOT?! THAT'S JUST WHAT I WANTED TO HEAR!

15

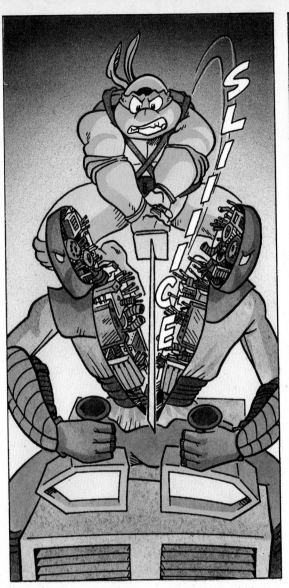

SEE? THERE'S NO BLOOD AT ALL...

NICE WORK, LEO!

...JUST A LITTLE OIL!

NOT FAR AWAY...

WE IS BACK, MISTA SHREDDA!

AND WE BRUNG YOU DAT CHAMELEON-GUY...

...BUT HE AIN'T GOT NO WEAPONS PLANS ON HIM!

16

17

18

ALL RIGHT. YOU'VE *CONVINCED* ME.

THE STOLEN PLANS ARE HIDDEN IN A SPACE BETWEEN SOME WALL BRICKS BACK IN THE SEWER CHAMBER YOUR FRIENDS HERE ABDUCTED ME IN.

EEK!

EXCELLENT! BEBOP, ROCKSTEADY-- RETRIEVE THE PLANS *IMMEDIATELY!*

CONSIDER US GONE!

HA! HA! HA!

YOU CAN *RELEASE* ME NOW, SHREDDER.

RELEASE YOU?

I WAS HOPING TO *CONVINCE* YOU TO *JOIN* ME...

19

I DOUBT IT.

HUH?
WHERE'D
HE GO?

BETTER MEN
THAN YOU HAVE
FAILED IN BATTLE
AGAINST ME!

DON'T
MESS
WITH
ME!

I KNOW
YOU'RE IN HERE
SOMEWHERE,
FOOL!

I'VE GOT IT JUST ABOUT FIGURED OUT...

I THINK I CAN RUN IT IF YOU NEED ME TO, LEO.

GREAT, DON.

COOL!

DON'T YOU THINK WE'VE HUNG AROUND HERE LONG ENOUGH? SHOULDN'T WE BE HEADING AFTER BEBOP AND ROCKSTEADY?

SURE, NOW THAT DON'S HAD HIS TIME WITH THE KNUCKLE-HEAD.

GREAT... I MEAN, THE TRAIL GROWS COLDER AS WE STAND HERE...

22

23

24

LOOKS LIKE A **STAND-OFF** FROM UP HERE:

THE TURTLE GUYS THROWING **SHURIKEN** FROM THE SAFETY OF THE TUNNEL DARKNESS...

BEBOP AND ROCK-STEADY FIRING THEIR **RAYGUNS** FROM BEHIND THE LEGS OF THE KNUCKLEHEAD...

NEITHER PARTY CAPA-BLE OF ACHIEVING AN **EDGE** OVER THE OTHER.

I'D SAY IT'S HIGH-TIME TO **BREAK** THEIR STAND-OFF...

DUH, WHAT'S DAT **GLOW**?

UH-OH.

...WITH A **COLORFUL**...

25

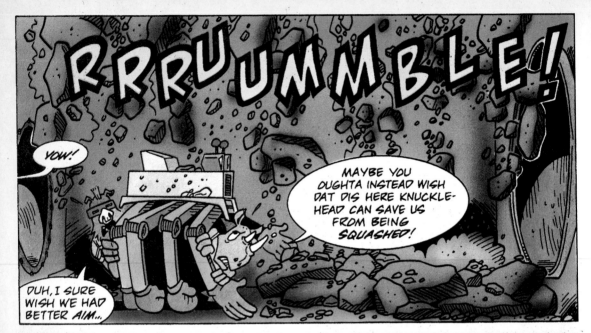

LATER:

--ARE STILL UNABLE TO DETERMINE WHAT CAUSED THE SECTION OF STREET TO COLLAPSE.

ELSEWHERE IN THE CITY, POLICE OFFICIALS HAVE CALLED OFF THEIR MANHUNT...

..FOR THE DOUBLE AGENT KNOWN AS CHAMELEON...

...AFTER THE SECRET WEAPONS PLANS THAT WERE STOLEN EARLIER TODAY WERE FOUND BURNT NEARLY BEYOND RECOGNITION...

..IN AN ENVELOPE DELIVERED TO THE UNITED NATION'S GENERAL SECRETARY THIS EVENING.

A NOTE WRITTEN ON THE OUTSIDE OF THE ENVELOPE IS REPORTED TO HAVE STATED:

"SOME THINGS ARE NOT WORTH PROFITING FROM."

THERE WAS NO EXPLANATION AS TO HOW SOMEONE WAS ABLE TO PASS IN AND OUT OF THE THEN-HEAVILY POLICED U.N. IN ORDER TO DELIVER THE NOTE...

SALE
26" COLOR DIAGONAL
279.95

NEATO MINI TV $99.95

...UNSEEN... OR AS TO WHY THE PLANS WERE FIRST STOLEN, AND LATER RETURNED.

SALE
26" COLOR DIAGONAL
279.95

NEATO MINI TV $99.95

YOU MIGHT SAY I'M BEGINNING TO SEE THINGS DIFFERENTLY NOW.

THE END!

ALL SORTS OF THINGS FIND THEIR WAY INTO A CITY'S *SEWERS.*

MANHATTAN'S SEWERS ARE A MELTING POT OF BOTH *NATURAL* AND *MAN-MADE SUBSTANCES.*

MANY OF THESE MAN-MADE SUBSTANCES ARE KNOWN TO BE *TOXIC* TO CREATURES AS DIVERSE AS THE HUMAN BEING...

...THE NORWEGIAN RAT...

...AND THE PLANARIAN FLATWORM.

THE UNCONTROLLED RELEASE OF MANY OF THESE TOXIC SUBSTANCES HAS BEEN MADE *ILLEGAL.*

HOWEVER...

GOING

DOWN?

PLOTTED BY DEAN CLARRAIN & RYAN BROWN
WRITTEN BY DEAN CLARRAIN
PENCILED BY KEN MITCHRONEY
INKED BY DAN BERGER
LETTERED BY GARY FIELDS

BUT OF COURSE, LEONARDO. WHAT IS IT YOU WISH TO ASK?

MASTER, RECENTLY SEVERAL *ODD EVENTS* HAVE HAPPENED TO US...

...AND SOME *PUZZLING THINGS* SAID.

INDEED, WARRIORS OF *GOOD*. MOURN NOT FOR LEATHERHEAD, FOR WHILE IT APPEARS YOU MAY HAVE LOST THIS CONFRONTATION, TAKE HEART IN THE KNOWLEDGE THAT IN THE *FINAL CONFLICT* VICTORY SHALL BE YOURS.

AND BEFORE WE HAD A CHANCE TO MOURN LEATHERHEAD, WE MET UP WITH HIM WRESTLING ON *STUMP ASTEROID*... WHERE HE CHOSE TO *REMAIN*.

HOLD IT! I DON'T WANT TO RETURN TO EARTH. I WANT TO *STAY*.

BACK ON EARTH I'M A *FREAK*; HERE I CAN BE A *HERO*.

I WONDER IF HE *TRULY* KNOWS WHAT IT TAKES TO BE A HERO?!

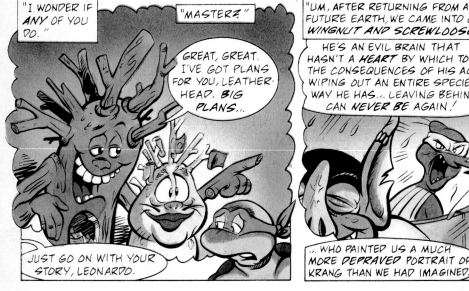

"I WONDER IF *ANY* OF YOU DO."

"MASTER?"

GREAT, GREAT. I'VE GOT PLANS FOR YOU, LEATHER-HEAD. *BIG PLANS*...

JUST GO ON WITH YOUR STORY, LEONARDO.

"UM, AFTER RETURNING FROM A GREENHOUSED FUTURE EARTH, WE CAME INTO CONFLICT WITH *WINGNUT AND SCREWLOOSE*..."

HE'S AN EVIL BRAIN THAT HASN'T A *HEART* BY WHICH TO WEIGH THE CONSEQUENCES OF HIS ACTIONS... WIPING OUT AN ENTIRE SPECIES THE WAY HE HAS... LEAVING BEHIND WHAT CAN *NEVER BE* AGAIN!

SOMEBODY'S GOTTA STOP HIM!

... WHO PAINTED US A MUCH MORE *DEPRAVED* PORTRAIT OF KRANG THAN WE HAD IMAGINED.

4

WHEN WINGNUT AND SCREWLOOSE TRIED TO ESCAPE, THEY WERE... WELL, *TAKEN*...

MISTER STUMP HAS SHOWN AN *INTEREST* IN THESE TWO... SO WE'RE OFF TO *STUMP ASTEROID*.

...BY *CUDLEY* THE COWLICK.

MISTER STUMP HAS HIS *PLANS*...

HMMM... THE EVENTS ALMOST APPEAR *RELATED*.

YES, MASTER.

LEONARDO, *WHAT* IS YOUR *QUESTION*?

THAT'S WHAT I SAID TWO HOURS AGO!

MASTER... WHAT CAN WE DO?

WHAT IS IT THAT BOTHERS YOU *MOST*?

THE *FINAL CONFL*—

NO. KRANG.

I CAN'T BELIEVE WHAT KRANG DID TO WINGNUT AND SCREWLOOSE'S SPECIES...

SO. YOU WISH TO STOP KRANG. *WHO* IS YOUR ONLY TANGIBLE *LEAD*?

THE... SHREDDER...?

IS THAT A STATE- MENT OR A QUESTION?

A STATE- MENT, MASTER.

GOOD. IT IS TIME TO SEARCH OUT KRANG. BEGIN BY LOCATING THE SHREDDER'S *HIDDEN LAIR*, SEE IF YOU CAN PICK UP ANY LEADS AT HIS *SUB BASE*.

5

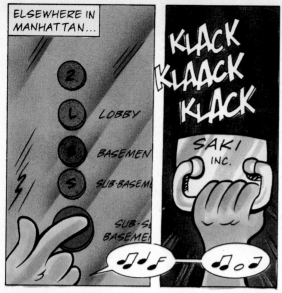

ELSEWHERE IN MANHATTAN...

2
L LOBBY
B BASEMEN
S SUB-BASEME
SUB-S
BASEMEN

KLACK
KLAACK
KLACK

SAKI
INC.

♪♪♫   ♪♫♩

NOW WHO COULD *THAT* BE? *BEBOP* AND *ROCKSTEADY* HAVE BEEN GONE FOR *DAYS*... BUT THEY'VE NEVER USED THE FRONT DOOR BEFORE...

PERHAPS IT'S *FINALLY* THE...

EXTERMINATOR!

YOU'RE *LATE*.

AIN'T WE ALL, PAL, AIN'T WE ALL. SUPPOSE YOU JUST TELL ME WHERE YOU NEED THE *SERVICE*, WHERE YOU GOT THE *ROACHES*.

THEY'RE IN THAT *STORAGE ROOM* OVER THERE.

JUST LOOK AT ALL THEM *VERMIN* RUN!

THIS MAY TAKE A GOOD *WHILE*...

I DON'T CARE *HOW* LONG IT TAKES, AS LONG AS YOU KILL THEM *ALL*. I *HATE* ROACHES!

SLAM!

STORAGE ROOM

DANGER!!

INSOLENT FOOL!

7

NOW LET'S SEE IF I CAN GET THROUGH TO *KRANG*...

SAKI?

YES, WE SEEM TO HAVE A *BAD CONNECTION,* KRANG.

THAT'S BECAUSE I'M IN *TRANSIT* BETWEEN *WORLDS*... OUR SIGNAL IS PROBABLY MEETING WITH INTERFERENCE FROM OTHER TRANSMISSION SIGNALS -- THIS *IS* A RATHER HEAVILY POPULATED SECTOR OF *DIMENSION X*...

OR AT LEAST IT *WAS*, HEH HEH. NOW... WHAT IS IT YOU *WANT*, FOOL?

ZICK

ZICK

SOMETHING, SAKI... SOMETHING THAT I *JUST KNOW* IS OUT THERE *SOMEWHERE*.

I MUST HAVE IT, AND I WILL LEAVE NO *STONE* UNTURNED IN MY SEARCH...

WANT? THAT'S THE SAME QUESTION I WANTED TO ASK OF *YOU*.

WHAT DO *I* WANT?

8

9

ELSEWHERE BENEATH MANHATTAN:

NOTHING.

MAYBE THE SHREDDER'S ABANDONED THIS SITE SINCE WE *SUNK* THE SUB HE KEPT DOCKED HERE...

HMMM... WE MAY NOT FIND ANY LEADS AFTER ALL.

THIS ISN'T AS BAD AS IT *SEEMS*, LEO.

RIGHT... AND SINCE BOTH OF THESE POINTS SOMEHOW INVOLVE THE SHREDDER, THEN WHY DON'T WE SCAN A STRAIGHT LINE BETWEEN HERE AND THERE AND SEE WHAT WE FIND?

SOUNDS LIKE A PLAN.

THEN LET'S DO IT!

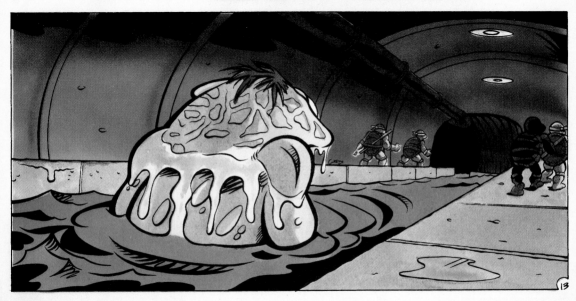

14

21

22

24

25

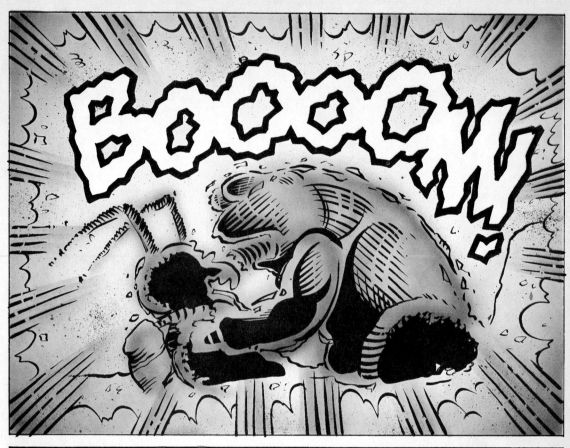

27

NEXT: OF RAT KINGS AND OTHER THINGS!